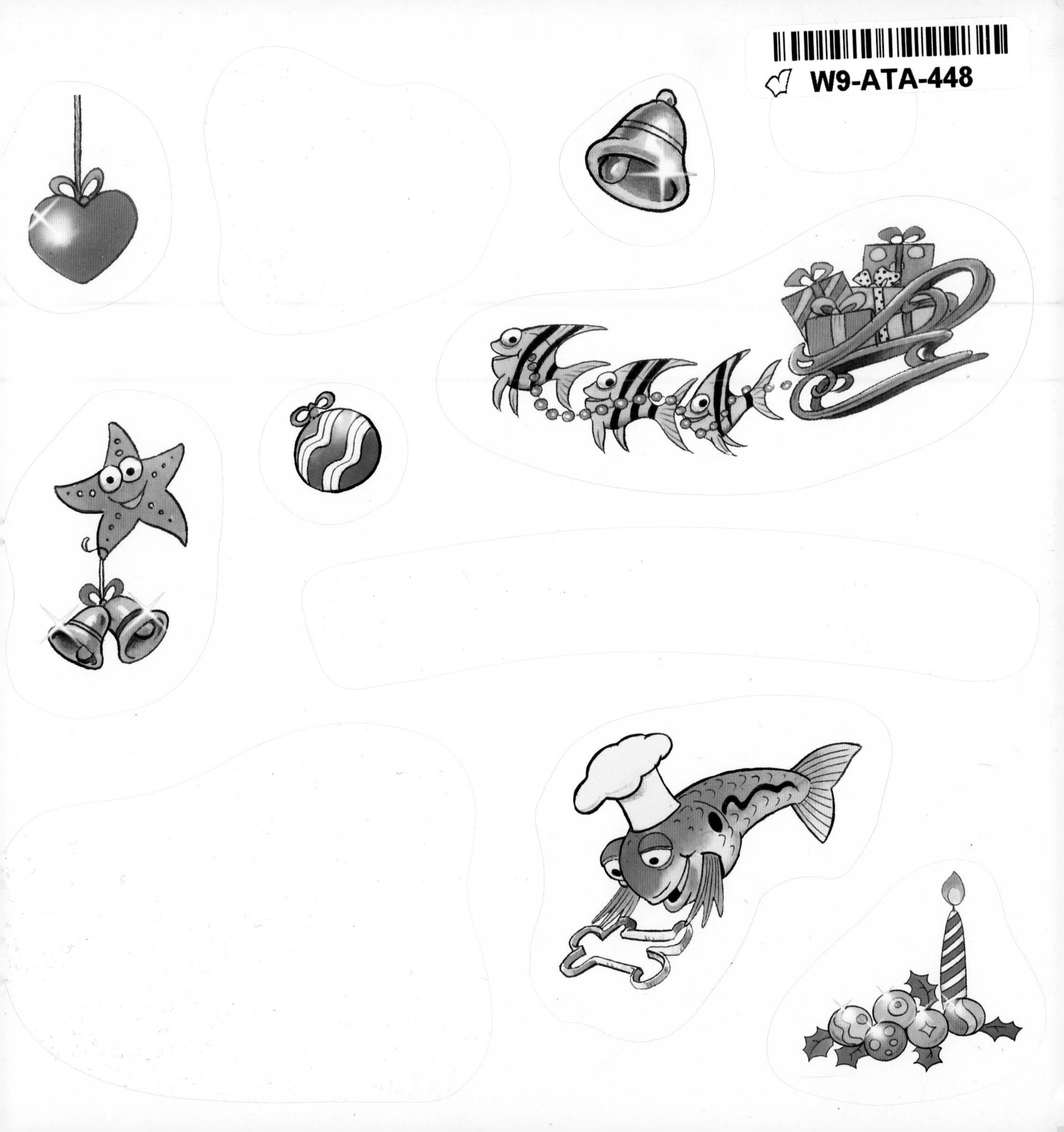

Pout-Pout Fish Christmas Spirit

Written by **Wes Adams** Illustrated by **Isidre Monés**

Based on the *New York Times*–bestselling Pout-Pout Fish books
written by Deborah Diesen and illustrated by Dan Hanna

Farrar Straus Giroux
New York

Farrar Straus Giroux Books for Young Readers
An imprint of Macmillan Publishing Group, LLC
120 Broadway, New York, NY 10271

Color separations by Embassy Graphics
Printed in China by RR Donnelley Asia Printing Solutions Ltd., Dongguan City, Guangdong Province
Designed by Aram Kim
First edition, 2019
10 9 8 7 6 5 4 3 2 1

mackids.com

Library of Congress Control Number: 2019931328
ISBN: 978-0-374-31048-6

Our books may be purchased in bulk for promotional, educational, or business use.
Please contact your local bookseller or the Macmillan Corporate and Premium Sales Department at
(800) 221-7945 ext. 5442 or by email at MacmillanSpecialMarkets@macmillan.com.

Christmas was coming, but Mr. Fish was not feeling jolly.

His friend Mr. Eight was preparing all sorts of sweets and treats.
"I need some holiday cheer," said Mr. Fish.
"I am sure you will cook up something," said the octopus.

Down in the deep, Mr. Fish found Mr. Lantern and his pals preparing a festive light show.

The dazzled Pout-Pout Fish was still in the dark about where to find what he needed.

Ms. Clam was teaching carols to a choir of angelfish.

Mrs. Squid had invited Starfish and his friend to decorate her coral Christmas tree.

Mr. Fish felt left out. Everyone else seemed to have a special way of showing Christmas spirit.

At Miss Shimmer's place, wherever he looked, Mr. Fish saw something bright and sparkly.

"Don't worry," said Miss Shimmer. "You will find a way to shine."

Mr. Fish was ready to give up his search when he swam by a big reef and discovered he wasn't the only creature needing a dose of holiday spirit.

A school of sardines swam by, and they all said they were hungry and looking for food.

A lonely crab said he wasn't in the holiday mood.

“I sprained a fin,” said a kind, old kingfish. “I could use some help with my decorations this year.”

In a flash, Pout-Pout Fish forgot his troubles and knew what he had to do.

One by one, he talked to all his friends. When they heard about those in need, everyone was happy to help. They brought food and lights, singers and decorations.

As he celebrated with his friends old and new, Mr. Fish bubbled with happiness.

"It seems you found your holiday spirit," said Miss Shimmer.

"I think it found *me*!" said Mr. Fish.

"MERRY CHRISTMAS, ONE AND ALL!"
Pout-Pout Fish cheered.